And Ampersand

And Ampersand

short stories on endings and beginnings (of a sort)

Ryan R. Campbell

A Cedarbrook Books Publication

Published by Cedarbrook Books
1817 Cedarbrook Lane
Stoughton, Wisconsin 53589
www.cedarbrookbooks.com

And Ampersand: Short Stories on Endings and Beginnings (of a Sort)

Printed in the USA
First Edition
March, 2020

eBook ISBN: 978-1-7363871-0-8

This book contains references or allusions to death, including suicide.

for you, before and after, always

Preface

What follows is rebirth.

It's the distillation of certainty from chaos, the culmination of careful contemplation and reckless devotion. It's the embrace of intuition over intellect, of emotion and approximation. It's sunrise coffee and footsteps on pavement, birdsong and blunder, woe at the hands of and triumph over oneself.

Here, together, we'll endure the shifting of the earth. We'll endure the sight of land after weeks at sea, its promise that the nascence of a new adventure oft accompanies the death of another.

To do this, we'll begin with endings.

To do this, we'll end with beginnings.

This should not be surprising. It's the natural order of things.

Here, together, we'll let this reality enfold us. It is the only one we have, and we endure it, every day, as we must.

So—

Welcome to rebirth. Welcome to the world.

Ryan R. Campbell, December 2020

And Ampersand

You die at twenty-four. Or twenty-one. Forty. Sixteen.

But you don't die overnight, not in the traditional sense. Your heart doesn't stop, your blood congeal, your body stiffen. The death of you comes on slowly; ageless, as steady as water's slow smoothing of stone. But when it happens, you know.

Your final breath escapes when the last of the magic leaves the world.

There are no more road trips. No co-pilot runs fingers through your hair. The windows are not rolled down because the car has been impounded, recycled into tin cans and barbed wire and children's playthings.

There are no more Christmas mornings. You, a child, do not wake, jubilant and unaware the true gift is to believe. Your family goes on, rises without you, unwrapping themselves on the living room floor.

Family, we're still family, they say, but it's all strings and shadowboxes and ampersands because symbols, darling, symbols and no words; the words can't mean anything if the magic is gone, so don't talk about it, talk about it, *don't*—

Despite this, they wonder about you. Sometimes. Fleetingly.

The magic is gone for them, too, though they pretend otherwise. They cling desperately to the idea of you—to the smell of you on a pillow or the sound of your laugh in a hall.

But these are figments; you're not there with them. You

haven't been and don't need to be.
    You died, you died, but the time to mourn has passed.
    Your life has only just begun.

Hello, My Name Is

He's never felt more alive than the moment before his death.

The engine roars as the vehicle careens over the turnpike's edge, below which eager waves await in a splashing, foamy tumult. Adrenaline tingles in his fingertips, sharpens his senses. Sea salt, seagull—their smells saturate the air, reminders of a life lived and that which is to come.

It's rushing to meet him now, the tide; he's left the windows open to invite it in. Soon, the crash. Seconds will bleed into eternity, his lungs clamoring, clamoring, clamoring for air, and then and then and then, *release*.

But he's not in the car. He wouldn't dare.

Did you see it, the spray of water? The empty driver's seat, the figure on the bluff overlooking the sea? He's watching, now, as his automobile salutes the light of the moon, gurgling, sinking, gone. He turns his back to this past, the one he's committed to the deep.

In the brush, another life awaits. He clears the foliage, his hands sticky with sweat and sap, and, yes, the car he's parked here remains at attention, its engine starved for life. Within, it's all accounted for: the duffel bag, the cash in the glove box, the maps.

The steering wheel is cold, but warms at his touch. He turns the key in the ignition. Pistons purr to life.

He's dead, this man, a version of him.

But here, now, he presses his foot to the accelerator, wondering at his name.

Glassed

My glass came on as if suddenly.

"Do you see it?" I asked.

"Stop fidgeting and ask him how he's doing."

With my arm extended, I stepped forward, backward, forward. There, still there. Always at arm's reach.

"You're doing it again."

So I ignored the glass, asked how he was doing, hugged when I was supposed to hug, which was not, it turned out, all of the time, even though *hugs, hugs, we're supposed to give hugs*.

Later, I walked. There had to be a corner, some confirmation of inside or out, but the glass proved without beginning or end. It proved impossibly high.

At times, others passed through it, unknowing. An arm around a shoulder, a pat on the back.

"You don't like it when people touch you."

I'm supposed to like it when people touch me. This is the same as hugs and not fidgeting and, as you tell me now, eye contact, but you're there, still there, whether I look or not.

And I'd rather not.

When I look, I see the glass. It's between us, always, even when part of you passes through, even when you insist it isn't there, are indifferent to that which *defines me*.

But one day, I wonder.

One day, I clean the glass.

I do this not because it has mildewed—no, it's as pristine as the day it first appeared, pretentious in its perfection. I clean the glass because if it's to define me, I must make it truly, unflinchingly mine.

So I clean the glass, and, at long last, recognize the glass is me, that I am glassed and not *with glass*.

I clean the glass knowing I'll see her, someday, a niece or second cousin or child of my own, tensing while wrapped in a hug, unable to hold one's gaze, to keep her fingers still.

I'll ask her then, if she sees it—the glass. Her glass. Our glass.

"You see it, too?" she'll ask.

And "Yes," I'll tell her. "Yes."

Thank You for the Fire

On the thirteenth day, all was surely lost.

The rain had seeped through to the marrow, his stomach howling with hunger.

Despite the relentless rush of rain against the side of the nylon tent, Brendan pressed his forearm against the flap to peer out over the valley.

The sky glowered in mean grays, the tops of the trees cowering. Even the tallest grass bowed, finally succumbing to the wrath of a hundred-year storm.

And rain. Rain, still.

Down the mud-steeped hillside, he spotted where he saw her last, the path he trod days earlier on his most recent search for her, the sinkholes yawning mere paces from where his boots had become stuck in the mud.

He saw, too, where they last built a fire.

She had wrapped her arms around him, that final night. The fire glowed before them, embers now where once a crackling blaze burned. "Just a little longer," she said, holding him tighter.

He told her it was late, that it had been for some time; they had a long hike ahead of them in the morning, too, with much to look forward to once it came to an end.

She released him from her hold. "I don't want it to end."

"It won't. Not now."

She inspected the ring once more. "It's going to take some time to get used to."

"We have the rest of our lives to get used to it."

"We do," she said. "We do."

Now, however, the fire pit had flooded, its charred contents long since washed down the hillside. Even if he were to find dry wood, he'd have to dig a new pit, which would require an even greater break in the rain. And strength—it would require a strength he hadn't known in the weeks since they set out.

Home, then. If the rain broke, he'd have to blaze a way home; the mudslide on the fourth night washed away the only trail, and even that had been a day's journey. Who knew how far the mudslide stretched or what dangers the now viscous earth held? Something had taken her, after all—unless, yes, and this is the thought he should have embraced all along: she was on the far side of the mudslide—of any sinkholes—when the hill sloughed its grassiest layer. She made it back, she did, and now it was only a matter of waiting to be found once the mountainside became passable again.

This faith did not endure.

Brendan cursed his lack of foresight. If only he'd brought further provisions—no, if only he'd brought his phone—no, if only he'd not let grief carry his search deeper into the forest.

He needed a fire—needed food—but could develop no plan for either. So he reclined instead, begging for reprieve. His eyelids grew heavy, his breathing slow, his extremities a ruinous blue.

Eventually, a popping sound roused him.

He lurched forward and cast open the tent's entrance, his eyes wild at the sight beyond.

A campfire. A growling, fearsome campfire.

Brendan inched his way from the tent to find the clouds broken in patches, a brilliant display of stars smiling upon him. There were no tracks in the mud, however, and no materials left behind. Whoever started this fire did so expertly and in total silence.

Brendan sidled up alongside the flames. They crackled with fury, melting away the cold of his fingertips, his toes. He would have inhaled the fire were he able, warming himself from within and using its strength to carry him home, to carry him to her if she'd somehow gone on living.

"You could do it, you know."

Brendan spun to find her standing over him, looming between him and his tent.

She stepped toward him, toward the fire, her voice impossibly sweet. "It's warm here—comfortable, without want." She gestured with a perfectly dry hand toward the flames. "I want this for you, Brendan. For us."

His jaw chattered too fiercely to respond.

"Watch." She held her hand to the fire—in the fire. "It's okay," she said. "Nothing to be done about it." After a pause, she stepped into it, consumed to the elbows in flame. "Please," she said. "Won't you join me?"

The warmth had already seeped up his forearms, had penetrated above the ankle. Even his nose had thawed, his brow able to wrinkle once more.

So he joined her—a hand at first, then an arm—expecting the smell of burning flesh, the searing pain of smoke in his lungs. Instead, a sizzle, a spark that popped and urged him further.

He climbed in, standing now. The flames cleansed him, licking at his hair, his heels, his hips, and the cinders within him flickered and spread, melting away the glacial pain that had taken his chest. His strength returned to him, his arms at last flexing with ease. "Thank you," Brendan said. "Thank you."

"Listen, now."

Brendan's eyes grew heavy, the fire raging around him.

It sounded like the windswept valley, like thunder clapping overhead.

It sounded like the pitter patter of rain on the roof of the nylon tent.

It sounded like birdsong, like water rushing, gently, downhill.

Brendan stirred and found himself reclined, naked, inside the tent, as warm as he'd ever been.

"I'm waiting, Brendan," her voice said. "Come find me."

And through the tent flap, sun.

State Line

Drivers from Illinois should be banned.

They do ninety in our seventies.

They never signal.

They kill my wife.

Now, the tendons of my fingers throbbing from my grip of the wheel, I lean forward. Powder falls softly, a tender November snow kissing the road. It's graceful, so graceful, until the wind cuts through the snow with a familiar swiftness: that of the sedan when it first appeared in our rearview mirror. From right lane to middle to left and back, he weaved, his brights scorching, icy pavement cracking beneath his tires.

My wife said something, a question I missed in my focus on the narrowing of lanes.

Before she repeated herself, he was on us, fishtailing into the rear of our vehicle. Tires squelched. My stomach, too. A scream, a roll, a slide. The thunder of a collision, the simultaneous whiplash. Silence. An awful, oppressive silence.

The funeral is this afternoon.

"Let us drive you," they said—family, friends. Naturally, I refused. The roads must be mine, will be mine again, and so I drive myself, park, and exit the vehicle alone.

Later, I stand over the casket. My jaw unclenches, and I pray for her, for myself, for the man who did this to her. I cannot, will not forgive him, not so long as her eyes remain closed, and yet, impossibly, I wish him well. I wish him a speedy recovery. I hope he finds himself whole, or as close to it as one can come, considering. I don't know if I wish these things on him as an act of release or with the hope he might suffer, living with the guilt. Regardless, for now, it's enough.

Later still, the bar. I want to be home, to be through with the *thank you for coming* and *I'll miss her dearly* and *a miracle, indeed*, even though escaping with a concussion is no miracle when one loses half of oneself in exchange.

They all would have left by now, too, were it not for the game. The Packers play on every screen, and I shouldn't be here; I should be watching with her at home: the crackle of a delicate fire, the cats lazing on our laps, the steady creep of the soft Sunday dread that comes only with the prospect of a new week ahead.

Instead, my elbows rest against the knotty, unpolished wood of the bar, and Rodgers throws a rare game-ending interception.

I'm in the parking lot, fists clenched.

Irritability, they say, is a symptom of the concussion, a symptom of grief, but this Jeep—parked half in one stall, half in another—stirs some deeper ire. Its license plate incenses, too, with its boastful Land of Lincoln declaration, its Chicago Bears frame a further mockery still.

"Take a picture," some drunk says, adding it'll last longer. He approaches the Jeep, fumbling with his keys, and stabs the driver's side door three times before he finds the keyhole.

Let him go. He'll make for one less on the road if he—well, no.

"Hey," I say.

He stops, one foot on the running board.

"Let me give you a ride."

The state line is mere miles from here, his home mere miles and one. We ride in a cool, relative silence, his whiskey-soaked breath billowing within my rental's never truly heated cabin.

A Durango—Illinois plates—passes on the left, sluicing through the slush as it zips back into the right lane and slams on the brakes at a red. My brakes lock. I slide. We stop inches from the Durango's bumper.

"Damn animals," the drunk says. "Oughta be banned."

"You, too, huh?"

"Eh?"

I shake my head, snicker as we cross the state line.

"Two more blocks," says the drunk, whose name I learn is Earl.

The light changes ahead. Green to yellow.

I brake.

Yellow to red.

I can't stop, won't stop in time.

Earl says something, a question I miss in my focus on pumping the brakes, on scanning for cross-traffic. A horn blasts to my left. My stomach bottoms out. An F-150 barrels for my door, and the truck's driver throws the steering wheel to the side. He skirts around us, tires screeching. A scream—this time, from me—but no roll, no slide. No collision. No whiplash.

But the silence. An awful, oppressive silence.

The F-150 surges down the road, a gloved finger flashed my direction through a specially rolled down window.

The light changes, red to green.

"Over," Earl says. "Pull over."

I do.

Earl exits, slams the door, and trudges the final block home on his own.

I check my mirrors, signal, make a U-turn.

Then, the tendons of my fingers throbbing from my grip of the wheel, I cross the state line, the roads mine again, my silent prayers those of release.

Backward from Ten

No godparent expects to become a guardian.

No godparent expects to raise their godchild as a single parent.

No godparent expects to be run through with rebar, the meat of their thigh howling as it hemorrhages, their vision blurring at the edges.

"Tell her," Russ pleads. "Tell her."

The foreman pats him twice on the arm.

"Who's the her?" asks a paramedic, transitioning Russ to the back of an ambulance.

The foreman covers his face with a gloved hand, turns away.

"I love her," Russ says in the back of the ambulance, its siren wailing. "Tell her I loved her as if she were my own kid. She was my kid."

"She *is* your kid. Will always be your kid." The paramedic maintains eye contact while she says it, and the blurring of Russ's vision slows. "You loved her. Do. Will."

Russ wishes he had said it with as much confidence as the paramedic.

His fingertips are cold now, his toes, too. The tip of his nose catches the chill next, and soon, Russ suspects, the cold will take him whole.

And to think—they never returned to the park.

"Push me," she shrieked, and he did. "Higher, higher." Her loose, golden curls fluttered in the wind, those tiny black dress shoes—unreasonable to wear to the park, but she insisted—reflecting the light of the setting sun.

"One more," Russ said, laughing along with her. "Then we have to go. It's getting dark."

"It won't get dark if you keep pushing," she said.

So he pushed her twice more, a third time, a fourth. Still, the darkness came.

"Another time," he promised her as she clicked her seatbelt into place. "We'll go another time."

"Soon?"

"Soon."

Soon came and went, and now, months—a full year?—later, Russ finds his lap sticky with blood, so much blood, and the hospital lights zoom past overhead, a heavenly glow about them.

Surgery, he hears. An operating room.

He wants to tell them no, that an operating room isn't where he's meant to be, that there's a park, the one on Glenway, and if someone could please pick her up and bring her; he's so terribly tired, but not too tired to push her once they're there.

"We're going to take care of this okay, Russell?" a doctor says. "But I need you to count backward from ten."

The doctor places a mask over Russ's nose and mouth, and it's warm, warmer than any part of him, and the awful taste of iron is finally chased from the air.

Ten, Russ counts, cursing his brother and sister-in-law for thrusting parenthood upon him.

Nine. Five more than died that day. Mother. Father. Daughter, in a way. Himself in the same.

Eight. He would perish here for a second time. She would, too, at the news.

Seven. He never told her he loved her because he could never be her real father, because she wouldn't have believed him.

Six. An immense weight impresses itself upon him. His legs are gone, his arms, too. He exists only in his mind, a tortured, grief-stricken point of light.

Five. If this is to be his forever, he can't let it be one of anguish, of misery.

Numbers four and three and two and one are lost. He gropes for joy in the void. A promise, a promise. The park on Glenway. This is where he should be, wants to be, and she can join him even if no one gives her a ride.

So Russ pushes her, the sun low in the sky, and she squeals and squeals and squeals. A warmth finds him, tingling in his toes and the tips of his fingers. His legs return, his arms. She flies from the swing, lands, and embraces him, thanks him, hugs him tight.

Then he lifts her by the underarms and returns her to the swing.

It can't get dark if he keeps pushing.

Yellow in the Deep

The pine needles prickled my feet, the golden sun flickering through the branches.

"Are you excited?" Mom asked.

Yes, of course, yes. Up ahead, the beach. Beyond, the lake—massive, far larger than any pool in which I'd swum.

"We're proud of you no matter what," Dad said.

But no, no *no matter what*. Win.

We entered the clearing, pine needles giving way to sand. Four dozen swimmers stretched, chatted, breathed deep, every last one of them in yellow, numbered caps.

My mother, insistently: "He's on the list somewhere."

A volunteer pored over a clipboard. My name, there, and yes, a cap of my own, rubber and yellow and tight to my scalp.

"Ooh, you're a real swimmer now," she said.

Not yet. Race first. Win.

In the shallow, the water ankle high, the crowd coalesced. Young, old, we'd swim together as one, our yellow caps gliding over the surface of the lake—and, amid churning waves—our numbers lost.

But not us, not truly. Not me. The yellow is so they can find us if—

A man waved a starter's pistol. One mile around the lake. Stay outside the buoys. In case of cramps, call for a lifeguard; they'll always be near in aluminum dinghies. And, please, wait for the signal.

He raised the gun. It went off.

Forward, we ran, splashing and wading and diving when, at last, the water rose high enough. Ankles caught knees caught elbows, but okay, I'm okay, and the yellow is so they can find me if—

Frigid, open water. The rhythm. Above, the puttering of a plane, the roar of the crowd. Below, the muted sounds of splishing, splashing, of my heart pounding. Finally, equilibrium. Up-and-under-glide-and-pull and up-and-under-glide-and-pull and don't-forget-to-breathe-and-pull.

A quick glance. Yellow ahead, but little of it.

Up-and-under-glide-and-pull and—

There are few my age among the yellow I pursue. Only one, perhaps.

Up-and-under-glide-and-pull and *win*.

Speed, with speed, and here on the right, a dinghy and its taunt of *if*, but push through it; push through and ignore the yellow beyond, ignore the yellow in the deep.

Below, the silence. Above, the shouting. Below, the nothing. Above, the silence.

Above. The silence.

A whistle cut through the quiet, echoed across the lake. Megaphones implored us out of the water, but yes, yes, a race is an attempt to exit first! With purpose now, purpose, but the speed with which some glide for shore, cheating by cutting across buoys and—*oh*.

The yellow, the yellow in the deep.

An elbow, they said. Or a knee. No one recalled a bump, a jostling, but it happened; there's no denying the lifeless body of a child salvaged from the murk, his ankles dragged through sand and pine needles, laid to rest on the shore.

Through the trees, the wail of an ambulance, a mother. Back, they said, back.

I removed my cap, clutched it tight.

"Are you okay? Come here," Mom beckoned.

We walked, then, to the car, a towel over my shoulders, water running in rivulets down my legs.

I trailed my parents, consumed with that which was behind me, yet horrified to advance. The silence. I longed for the quiet beneath the waves, but even there I would find no reprieve.

When we passed a receptacle in the lot, I discarded the yellow cap.

Swim, swim on, but swim no more forever.

A Final Gift

They're only jackets, I tell myself, heaving the bag from the closet floor. I've seen them countless times on his shoulders; it will be nothing—*nothing*—to pull them out, to try them on, to make two separate piles.

Keep what you like. Donate the rest.

Here, a breath. The overturning of the bag. The work begins.

First, the windbreaker,
the bomber,
the blouson,
the snowblower and the
it's damn cold and these dogs need a walk.

Now, shivering in the sweatshirt I wore before the work began, I stand before the mirror with one pile—*keep*.

For however long I wear these jackets, I'll have my father unloading his truck in the rain;
chest puffed, shoulders squared;
taking my mom on a date;
knee-deep in snow on the driveway;
grumbling his way through the walking of those dogs;
and through it all, my shoulders snug where his once were, enveloped in his embrace.

Acknowledgments

Books are often written in solitude, but infrequently are they published that way.

I'm indebted to feedback from early readers like Dan Schiro, Madolyn Rogers, Jason Guy, Rick Richards, and Chuck Ogg. I'm especially grateful for the input of Kathryn Keener, Avery Ames, Naomi Ansano, Audely Bensen, Alicia, and Jaedyn.

About the Author

Ryan R. Campbell lives in Stoughton, Wisconsin, with his wife, Lacey, and their cats, Hashtag and Rhaegar. Together, they own and operate Kill Your Darlings Candle Company, which sustainably illuminates the lives of readers, writers, and their communities with their candles for the wordsmiths of the world.

The author's work as R.R. Campbell has earned him accolades including finalist placement in the International Book Awards and acclaim from *New York Times* bestselling authors.

He is the founder of the Writescast Network and a member of the board of directors for the Wisconsin Writers Association. Previously, he taught for the University of Wisconsin's Division of Continuing Studies in Writing, and he is a regular speaker at conferences throughout Wisconsin and beyond.

for more

ryanrcampbell.com

Twitter: @iamrrcampbell
Instagram: @iamrrcampbell
Facebook: facebook.com/iamrrcampbell
Twitch: twitch.tv/hence_fort

Other books by this author
(published as R.R. Campbell)

Accounting for It All

The EMPATHY Sci-Fi Saga
Imminent Dawn
Mourning Dove